A Good Day for Clifford

by Janelle Cherrington

Illustrated by Isidre Mones

Based on the books by Norman Bridwell

D1264511

SCHOLASTIC INC.

New York Toronto London Auckland Sydney
Mexico City New Delhi Hong Kong Buenos Aires

Clifford, Cleo, and T-Bone ran on the beach.

But Clifford tripped and fell.

Clifford stood up and shook.

Then he felt it.

"I cut my foot!" he said.
T-Bone and Cleo took
a look.

Cleo said, "That does not
look good.
Let's get Emily Elizabeth."

Emily Elizabeth and Charley also took a look at Clifford's foot.
It had a deep cut in it.

Charley said, "That does not look good."

"We need a vet's help," Emily Elizabeth said.

Dr. Dihn took a look.

"Clifford needs stitches," she said.

"And he also needs a lot of rest.
Keep him inside. He cannot run and play."

Clifford was very sad.

He did not want to rest, but his foot felt bad.

Emily Elizabeth petted him.

She hugged him.

She even cooked him a big bone.

"Cheer up, Clifford!"
Emily Elizabeth said.

"I know you want to
run and play.

But we can still have fun.

We can read a book!"

So Emily Elizabeth read one of Clifford's favorite books.

Clifford's foot even felt a little better.

"Nothing helps you feel better than rest and a good book," said Emily Elizabeth.

It was a good day for
Clifford after all.